# Brad's Birthday Cake

Story by Dawn McMillan    Illustrations by Pat Reynolds

Rigby®

A Harcourt Achieve Imprint

www.Rigby.com
1-800-531-5015

"Look, Grandma," said Ella.

"I can see Brad outside his house."

"Hello, Brad," she called.

Grandma said hello to Brad, too.

Brad came over to the fence.

"Hello, Mrs. Scott. Hello, Ella,"

he said.

"It's my birthday on Sunday.

I'm going to be seven.

Will you come

to my birthday party, Ella?"

"Yes, please," said Ella.

On Saturday morning
Ella said to Grandma,
"I want to make a present for Brad.
Can we make him
a surprise birthday cake?"

"Yes," said Grandma,

"let's make the cake now."

The next day Grandma said,
"I will get the birthday candles."

"We can't put candles
on Brad's cake," said Ella.
"He won't see them."

"You are right," said Grandma.

"There are some big peppermints
left in this bag!" said Ella.
"Let's put them on Brad's cake.
He can't see candles,
but he can smell peppermints."

"Clever girl!" said Grandma.

Grandma iced Brad's cake,
and Ella put seven peppermints
on top.

Ella took the cake
to Brad's house.

13

"Happy birthday, Brad," said Ella.
"Grandma and I made you
a surprise birthday cake."

"Thank you!" said Brad.
"I can smell peppermints
on my cake!"

"Yes," said Ella, "and I made a 7 with seven big peppermints!"